Matthew A.   Matthew B.   Matthew C.

Peter Catalanotto

Matthew A.B.C.

Aladdin Paperbacks
New York London Toronto Sydney

Matthew — Always
Be
Creative!

2013

For Esmé

ALADDIN PAPERBACKS

An imprint of Simon & Schuster Children's Publishing Division

1230 Avenue of the Americas, New York, NY 10020

ALADDIN PAPERBACKS and colophon are registered trademarks of Simon & Schuster, Inc.

Also available in an Atheneum Books for Young Readers hardcover edition.

Designed by Michael Nelson

The text of this book was set in Lemonade Bold.

The illustrations were rendered in watercolor.

Manufactured in China 0213 SCP

First Aladdin Paperbacks edition July 2005

10 9

The Library of Congress has cataloged the hardcover edition as follows:

Catalanotto, Peter.

Matthew A.B.C. / Peter Catalanotto.

p. cm

"A Richard Jackson book."

Summary: A boy named Matthew joins Mrs. Tuttle's class, which already has twenty-five students whose first

names are Matthew and whose last names begin with every letter except Z.

ISBN 978-0-689-84582-6 (hc.)

[1. Names, Personal—Fiction. 2. Identity—Fiction. 3. Schools—Fiction. 4. Alphabet] I. Title.

PZ7.C26878 Mat 2002

[E]—dc21 2001022986

ISBN 978-1-4169-0330-7 (pbk.)

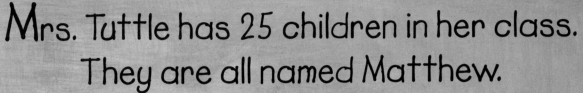

Mrs. Tuttle has 25 children in her class.
They are all named Matthew.

Principal Nozzet wonders how Mrs. Tuttle tells them apart.

She finds it quite simple.

Bb

Matthew B. loves Band-Aids.

Matthew C.
has friendly cowlicks.

Cc

Ee

Matthew E. forgets how to eat.

Ff

Matthew F. has a cat on his face.

Matthew I.
is incognito.

Jj

Matthew J.
works a night job.

Matthew K.
is unusually fond of ketchup.

Kk

Ll

Matthew L.
leaks.

Nn

Matthew *N.* is nearly naked.

Matthew O.
stays outside.

Pp

Matthew P. is perpetually perplexed.

Qq

Matthew Q.
is queasy.

Rr

Matthew R.
is freckled with a rhinoceros.

Ss

Matthew S.
can't wait for summer.

Uu

Matthew U. is completely uneven.

Vv

Matthew V.
is constantly volunteering.

Matthew W.
has a very high waist.

Matthew X. swallowed the xylophone.

Matthew Y. only yodels.

SHOW AND ~~TELL~~
YODEL

Principal Nozzet tells Mrs. Tuttle
she has a new student.

His name is . . .

Matthew.

Zz

Mrs. Tuttle sees he is
exactly what her class needs.

MATTHEW ZEE